ALL THIS
AND MORE

ALL THIS AND MORE

Written and illustrated by Ben Treanor.

To Mia and Finn.

You are all of this and more.

Little bear sat up
while tying his shoe,

And asked
'How much do I mean to you?'

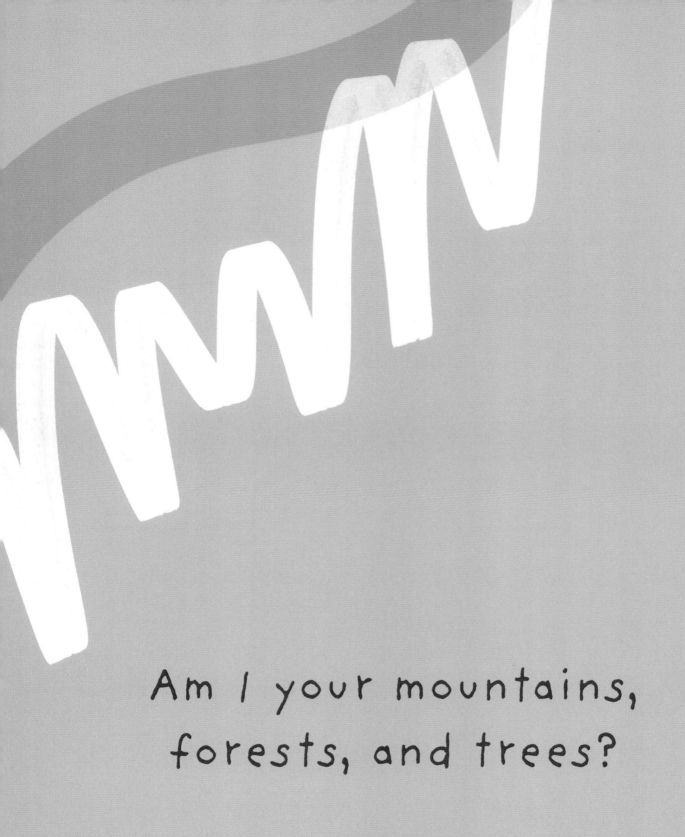

Am I your mountains, forests, and trees?

Am I your blustery winds
and light cool breeze?

Am I your space,
stars, and moon?

Am I your springtime months,
April, May and June?

Am I your rivers and winding streams?

Am I your rain, clouds,
and warm yellow sunbeams?

Am I your deep oceans
with all of the fish?

Am I your bed time stories, hugs, and good night kiss?

Big bear stood tall
and picked little bear
up off the floor,

'You, little bear,
are all of this...
and much, much more'.

Printed in Great Britain
by Amazon